# THE
# *Christmas Mouse*

## by Robin Crichton
### Abridged by Marjory Purves

## Illustrated by Val Biro

Ladybird

Karl Maraucher was one of the finest organ builders in Austria. He travelled all over Europe, mending old organs and putting in new ones.

In his workshop high up in the mountains were some very special musical mice, known as mouseorganists. Each Maraucher organ had a mouseorganist to look after it.

In the spring of 1818, when the snow had melted, Karl set off for Germany with a wagonload of spare parts.

Peeping out from the wagon covers was a

# Silent Night

Still the night, holy the night!
Sleeps the world; hid from sight,
Mary and Joseph in stable bare
Watch o'er the Child beloved and fair,
    Sleeping in heavenly rest,
    Sleeping in heavenly rest.

Still the night, holy the night!
Shepherds first saw the light,
Heard resounding clear and long,
Far and near, the angel-song,
    'Christ the Redeemer is here!
    Christ the Redeemer is here!'

Still the night, holy the night!
Son of God, O how bright
Love is smiling from thy face!
Strikes for us now the hour of grace,
    Saviour, since thou art born!
    Saviour, since thou art born!

For Edward and David Dorrell
with special thanks to many people in
Arnsdorf, Oberndorf, and Hallein,
and Jocelyn Stevenson for some of
the best lines.

British Library Cataloguing in Publication Data

Purves, Marjory
  The Christmas mouse.
  I. Title    II. Crichton, Robin    III. Biro, Val    IV. Series
  823.914[J]
  ISBN 0-7214-1420-6

First edition

Published by Ladybird Books Ltd  Loughborough  Leicestershire  UK
Ladybird Books Inc  Auburn  Maine 04210  USA

© in presentation LADYBIRD BOOKS LTD MCMXCI
Story used under licence from Edinburgh Film and Video Productions.

Printed in England (7)

little mouse. She was called Nonny the Nonentity, because she was so little and shy. Now, she had decided to go out into the world and become someone special.

One Monday morning, Karl arrived with his wagon at St Nikola's Church in Laufen, where a very old, very clever mouse looked after the organ.

Father Nostler, the priest of St Nikola's, came out to meet Karl. The priest was a bad-tempered old man, and everyone called him Patter Nostler, because he talked so much.

Nonny jumped down and scurried into the church. "Fay! Fay Mouse!" she squeaked, as she climbed into the organ loft.

But there was no reply. Fay Mouse had gone to the Great Organ in the sky. There was nobody to look after this organ now.

"I will have to do it," thought Nonny. She started to check the organ the way she had been taught.

Outside, Patter and Karl were arguing. Patter wouldn't let Karl start work until the organist was there to watch. And since the organist was also a schoolteacher, he couldn't come until the weekend.

"Perhaps Joseph Mohr, the curate, could watch me," suggested Karl.

But Patter wouldn't agree to that, because he didn't like Joseph. Everyone else liked Joseph, because he was jolly.

While the two men argued, Nonny went on
checking the organ. It was in a terrible state
and the bellows were worn out. When she had
finished, there was still no sign of Karl.

She looked down into the church, then outside – and realised with a fright that Karl and the wagon had gone. She ran down the street, looking for him. But there was no sign of Karl or the wagon.

Suddenly a shadow loomed, and a big black cat jumped at her. She ran as fast as she could, but the cat came closer and closer. Only a miracle could save her.

And it did! "Shoo! Pick on someone your own size!" said a little boy, scooping up Nonny in his hand.

"Hullo, Mouse! Are you all right?" he asked. Nonny was too tired even to squeak. Then everything went black as she fainted.

When Nonny came to, she was in a cage.
She put her nose to the bars to look outside.
She was in a classroom!

"Father! My mouse is alive!" said a voice
nearby. It was Felix, the little boy who had
saved her!

The next minute, Nonny was surrounded by
children. "Off you go! Class dismissed," said
the teacher, who was also Felix's father. "The
little mouse is going to live, so don't frighten
her to death!"

Then everybody had gone except Felix and his father, Franz. As Felix picked up the cage, Nonny promised herself that one day she was going to repay his kindness.

Felix's mother came in. "You two had better leave for Laufen right now! You know Patter Nostler doesn't like people to be late," she said.

"I hope the organ mender gets to Laufen before the organ breaks down!" said Franz as he put on his coat.

"Yes," agreed Felix. "I have to pump the bellows harder than I used to!"

Organ mender! Laufen! Bellows – the ones that were about to fall apart at St Nikola's Church! Now it all made sense to Nonny. She ran round the cage, banging the bars. She had to get out.

"Let her out now that she is better," said Felix's mother. "Wild creatures are happier outside."

Felix took Nonny from the cage and put her in his pocket. Then he set off for Laufen with his father.

When they were well on their way, Felix put Nonny down on the ground. "You're free now, little mouse!" he said, sad to let her go.

But Nonny followed them. After all, she was a mouseorganist and her place was in the church at Laufen.

"I don't suppose Patter will notice one more churchmouse," chuckled Felix's father, as they went into St Nikola's.

The months passed and soon the winter snow began to fall. Every Sunday Felix came to pump the bellows. He always brought something tasty for Nonny, and they became good friends.

Felix told Nonny of his dream that one day he would go to the Music School in Salzburg. He longed to be a great musician like his father.

Franz wrote wonderful music, but if the old priest didn't like the music he wrote, it was put away and never played again.

Nonny was no longer a Nonentity – she was now official mouseorganist at St Nikola's Church. It was hard work, however, and very worrying. As soon as she patched one hole in the bellows, two more appeared. Karl Maraucher would not come now until next spring, when the snow melted. Nonny just had to keep the bellows going until he came back.

One day, Nonny watched as some women
put a crib with a baby and a manger on one of
the altars, and decorated the church.
Something special was happening!

Next morning, Felix ran upstairs and held out a really tasty-looking sausage. "It's your Christmas present," he explained. Nonny had no idea who Chris Mouse was, but she was delighted with her sausage.

Franz sat down at the organ and began to play. The bellows began to stretch and... oh, no! Nonny saw that one of her largest patches was coming off.

Whatever could she do? Quickly she pushed her sausage into the hole. Would it hold?

She had no time to find out, because Patter Nostler ordered Franz and Felix downstairs. Nonny hopped quickly into Felix's pocket.

Patter thought Joseph the curate was going to be late, although there was still plenty of time. "We'd have no Christmas if we relied on him," he grumbled. "Send the boy to fetch him from the tavern."

It was the first time Nonny had been outside the church since the day she came back with Felix, and she was enjoying herself.

Long before they reached the tavern, she could hear singing. Inside, it was dim and smoky, but people were laughing happily. They clapped as Joseph played the last chords on his guitar. He looked up and saw Felix. "You've come to drag me back, haven't you?" said Joseph, rising to his feet with a smile.

By the time the three of them reached the church, Nonny was tired. She decided to have a nap in the bellows box.

Franz and Joseph sat down at the organ, and Felix began to pump the bellows.

Suddenly there was a loud "Plop!" and Nonny was knocked over by – a flying sausage!

And there was a huge hole where the sausage had been. It was all her fault. She had failed in her job, thought Nonny miserably. There'd be no organ music *this* Christmas.

Franz and Joseph sat in the vestry, looking sad. Felix was huddled in the corner with Nonny in his pocket. "How can we have Christmas without music?" said Franz.

Then Nonny had an idea – but she would have to be quick. Joseph's guitar was hanging on the door. The next second there was a crash as it toppled onto the floor, followed by Nonny, squeaking and running round in circles.

"I think my mouse is trying to tell us something," said Felix.

Joseph paid no attention as he stared thoughtfully at the guitar.

"Franz, why don't we have guitar music tonight?"

"A guitar? In church?" Franz was astonished.

"I've even got a little poem," said Joseph. "It goes —

> *Still the night, holy the night!*
> *Sleeps the world; hid from sight,*
> *Mary and Joseph in stable bare*
> *Watch o'er the Child beloved and fair,*
> *Sleeping in heavenly rest."*

"It *is* lovely," said Franz, "but Patter Nostler will never let us play a guitar in church."

"Well, don't mention the guitar. Just say that we are going to sing a carol," replied Joseph. "You could write the music. Then we could rehearse with the children of the choir before the service."

"You know Patter won't like it," Franz protested again.

"No, but *He* might," said Joseph pointing up to heaven.

That afternoon it started to snow. Franz sat at the harmonium in his music room, struggling to write a tune. He couldn't get further than the first two lines. When Felix came in with a cup of coffee, Franz took it to the window and the two of them gazed out.

*Happy Holidays from your Library*

Everything was white, and they could hear the bells ringing.

"Isn't it beautiful!" said Franz.

But Nonny was thinking more about the tune. Franz was not getting on very quickly. She decided to help.

Very carefully, Nonny dipped her paw into the inkwell and printed her mark on the music score. It looked quite good, so she did it again and again. Soon she had made little patterns all over the paper.

Suddenly Franz turned round and Nonny scampered off. "Oh, Felix!" Franz exclaimed. "Just look what your mouse has done!"

He was just about to throw the paper away when Felix cried, "Wait a minute! There's a pattern! E, E... is that C? Try it!"

"Don't be silly, Felix!" said his father, but he tried the notes on the harmonium all the same. Then he played the first four lines together. "That's amazing!" he exclaimed.

Nonny was almost as surprised as Franz when she heard her first attempt at writing music. She could hardly wait for the midnight service. It was going to be wonderful after all, even without the organ.

The church glowed with the light from a hundred candles when people began to arrive towards midnight.

Nonny watched from the organ loft as the old priest read the lesson. When it came to an end with "and on Earth peace, goodwill towards men," the children of the choir came in, led by Joseph with his guitar.

Everybody looked surprised. Patter could see the choir, but not Franz and Joseph, who stood beneath his pulpit.

As soon as Patter heard the guitar, he raised his hands to stop what was happening. Too late! The people were caught up in the magic of the music.

Then the service was over. Patter Nostler did not wish anyone a Happy Christmas. He marched straight off to the vestry and sent for Franz and Joseph.

Patter Nostler was very angry. "How dare you bring a guitar into my church, and turn the service into a sing-song!" he shouted.

"Joseph Mohr, you are finished! And as for you, Franz Gruber, you'd better stick to organ music from now on! But we won't need you until the organ is mended."

He crumpled Franz's piece of music into a ball, threw it into a corner and stormed out.

Joseph and Franz looked at each other sadly, then followed him.

Felix and Nonny had been listening outside the door. Felix had tears in his eyes and Nonny was sad too. If she'd been doing her job properly, this would never have happened. She would have to put things right.

She pushed Franz's piece of music under the music chest to keep it safe until she had a plan.

Time passed slowly. Joseph had gone to a parish up in the mountains, and the happenings of Christmas Eve were almost forgotten.

The days seemed long to Nonny with no organ to look after.

Then one morning in May, she heard Karl Maraucher's voice. She was so happy to see him. Franz and Felix were there to meet him this time, and her old friend E. Norm Mouse was in Karl's bag. Soon Norm was giving Nonny all the news from home.

Karl set to work on the organ and before long the floor was covered with spare parts.

Franz chatted to him as he worked, and told him all about the guitar in church.

"I'd like to hear the carol that caused so much trouble!" said Karl.

"I don't think I can remember it," replied Franz. "Patter threw away the piece of music, and I've tried to forget about it."

This was the moment Nonny had been waiting for.

She ran around squeaking to attract Felix's attention, then rushed downstairs towards the vestry. Felix followed her, wondering what was the matter.

There was no sign of Nonny in the vestry, but suddenly a crumpled ball of paper rolled out from underneath the music chest. It was the song that Franz had written!

Felix and Nonny raced back to the organ loft. "Look what my mouse has found!" said Felix.

"That *is* amazing," grinned Karl. He hummed the first few notes, then played the song on the organ. "I like it!" he said. "May I make a copy of it?"

"No, no, just take this one," insisted Franz,
"It's caused too much trouble already."
Nonny couldn't believe her ears! Franz was
giving away his song.

Quickly she explained to Norm how
important this song was. They decided there
and then to make sure that all the humans in
the world would hear it.

When Norm arrived home, he told the other mouseorganists about Franz's song.

They thought long and hard, and at last arranged for the song to reach a family of singers called the Rainers.

The Rainers travelled to many countries, and the organ they took with them had been built by Karl Maraucher. And of course they had a mouseorganist – Mag Nanny Mouse.

She was told to make sure that "Silent Night" was always there when the singers needed an extra song.

Franz's song was sung all over Europe in palaces, churches, concert halls and inns. The Rainers even took it with them when they travelled to America.

Other singers began to sing the song in *their* concerts.

Everywhere it was heard, people liked it and sang it too – in their homes and wherever songs were sung. At last "Silent Night" was known all over the world, as the mouseorganists had hoped.

The years passed. Felix became a young man, and went to study at St Peter's Music School in Salzburg.

Nonny gave up her job at St Nikola's, and moved to Salzburg with him.

One day Franz came to visit them, and Felix took his father to a little music shop that he'd discovered.

Suddenly Franz exclaimed, "Goodness me!" Nonny popped her head out of Felix's pocket. There in the middle of a book of songs was "Silent Night". It was in print at last! Now it would never be forgotten.

"They didn't get all the notes right. And it says Author Anonymous," frowned Felix.

Nonny wondered why her name was on it. She'd only helped a little bit. "You must write and tell them the truth, Father," said Felix.

But Franz shook his head. He had never had a high opinion of his own work.

Nonny couldn't understand why he wouldn't do anything about it. What could she do now?

Then she noticed a poster near the shop door. A concert was being given by singers called the Strassers – and "Silent Night" was one of the songs they were going to sing.

She couldn't make Franz go to the concert, so she would just have to go herself.

On the night of the concert, Nonny sat under the chair of an important-looking gentleman in the front row.

When the Strassers sang "Silent Night", the man turned to the lady next to him. "Excuse me, madam, I am the Royal Choirmaster in Berlin," he whispered. "Do you know who wrote this little carol? It would be perfect for His Majesty's Christmas Concert!"

"I think Michael Haydn wrote it," the lady replied, "but Father Ambrosius at the Music School will know. He has all Haydn's music."

Perhaps if she waited in the Music School library, the Royal Choirmaster would come, thought Nonny.

But weeks went by and nothing happened.

Then one day a letter arrived from Berlin, asking about the carol. Father Ambrosius groaned. It was going to take days to look through all the music written by Michael Haydn. He would ask one of the students to do it.

But when Father Ambrosius asked for help, not one student stood up. Not even Felix!

Nonny did the only thing that a mouse can do. She ran up Felix's trouser leg. "Ooh! Aah!" cried Felix, jumping up.

"Good! Come here, Felix," said Father Ambrosius. He handed him a rough copy of a song.

As soon as Felix looked at it he knew what it was. "I'm sorry, Father, but Michael Haydn didn't write this song. My father, Franz Gruber, wrote it — with a little help from a friend."

# POSTSCRIPT

Some time later, Franz wrote to the Royal Choirmaster. He sent the music score of "Silent Night" and told the story of how the carol came to be written.

That Christmas, the Royal Choir sang it for His Majesty the King of Prussia.

And it was sung every Christmas after that.

Since then, the beautiful carol has been translated into over a hundred different languages. On Christmas Eve during the American Civil War, and again during the Great War in 1914, the soldiers on both sides sang it together, bringing peace for just a few moments.

Franz Gruber and Joseph Mohr became famous, and everyone forgot about miserable old Patter Nostler.

Part of the town of Laufen became known as Oberndorf, and Joseph's guitar is still in the museum there. Every Christmas Eve it is taken out and played when "Silent Night" is sung.

This is mostly a true story. But until now, no one ever knew about Nonny – except Felix of course!

43

# Silent Night

Still the night, holy the night!
Sleeps the world; hid from sight,
Mary and Joseph in stable bare
Watch o'er the Child beloved and fair,
    Sleeping in heavenly rest,
    Sleeping in heavenly rest.

Still the night, holy the night!
Shepherds first saw the light,
Heard resounding clear and long,
Far and near, the angel-song,
    'Christ the Redeemer is here!
    Christ the Redeemer is here!'

Still the night, holy the night!
Son of God, O how bright
Love is smiling from thy face!
Strikes for us now the hour of grace,
    Saviour, since thou art born!
    Saviour, since thou art born!